CRIES IN HER SLEEP

Tribulations and Triumphs of Kiowa Artist Dolores Hummingbird

MW Ashe

ARCHER TRENT, PUBLISHER

The image on the front cover is by Robert Henri. The title is *Bernardita.* The original painting hangs in the San Diego Museum of Art. The image on the back cover is also by Robert Henri. The title of that painting is *An Irish Girl.*

Large-Print Edition
ISBN: 978-1-7347814-1-0

Dolores Hummingbird (AKA Cries in her Sleep) and Brenda Murphy (AKA Sky Eyes) are fictional characters, as are Chaplain Vance, Clovis Oliphant, David, and Benedict. All other named characters are actual historical figures and are portrayed here as accurately as diligent research has made possible.

For Alistair, Giles, and Trevor

CHAPTER 1

CARLISLE INDIAN INDUSTRIAL SCHOOL

Her birth name, as recorded by the Kiowa, Wichita, and Caddo Agency of Oklahoma, is *Dolores Hummingbird*. Under this, her proper Christian name, she was enrolled at the Carlisle Indian Industrial School. To the girls in her dormitory, however, she was known as *Cries in her Sleep*. She is of the Kiowa Nation, and she is my very best friend in all the world. This is her story.

My own birth name, by the way, is *Brenda Murphy,* but the Indian children secretly called me *Sky Eyes,* for the obvious reason that my eyes are blue. I am not Native American, you see, but Irish. I was born at the Carlisle Indian Industrial School, where my mother was a kitchen supervisor. She and I had rooms on campus, my father, a police constable, having been killed in the line of duty whilst I was yet in the womb.

When I was of an age to commence my formal education, I was initially enrolled in a public school in nearby Carlisle, Pennsylvania, but there I suffered, at the hands of my fellow students, such torments for being red-haired and freckled and for speaking with a foreign accent that eventually I was allowed to remain at home, attending classes with the Indian children. I cannot even imagine what negotiations my mother had to go through in order to accomplish that miraculous concession from her employers. In later years, there would be a number of Black scholars at the school, but I was the only White child ever to attend.

During my third academic year, typhoid fever swept through the school and claimed several lives, including that of my mother. Had I, at the time, given the matter any thought, I might reasonably have expected to be sent to an orphanage. Instead, becoming a ward of the school, I was moved into the new girls' dormitory. That was when I first became acquainted with Cries in her Sleep.

Recently arrived at the school, she was having a really difficult time adjusting to her new life. One of the youngest children ever enrolled at Carlisle, she had never before spent a single night away from home. She missed her parents terribly. My heart went out to her, and I devoted myself to helping her to feel not quite so alone and not so unbearably miserable. Somehow, my efforts in her behalf made it a little easier for me to endure my own grief.

There is probably a lesson in that, but I do not know how to put it into words. I know what Chaplain Vance would say though: "Now, that'll preach, brother. That'll preach." I have heard him speak those very words a hundred times or more.

Vance was one of several Dickinson College professors that served the Indian School as pastors. He was a very likeable man, but his theology (mainstream Protestant, as far as I know) was, to my mind, totally absurd. There is no system of belief so ridiculous that millions cannot be persuaded to embrace it. My mother, an atheist herself, had always encouraged me to think free and to be leery of any variety of orthodoxy. From a very young age, I viewed all established religions with extreme skepticism.

Oh, but that is off the subject. I was telling you about my earliest relationship with Dolores Hummingbird, otherwise known as *Cries in her Sleep*. I was nine years old when we met, tall for my age. She was younger by two and a half years and tiny. No one thought that she looked old enough to be in school. I believe most people would have guessed our age difference to be five or six years, for I towered over her.

And yet, our friendship seemed to be written in the stars. From the very beginning, we each felt a powerful affinity for the other. A deep and lasting sense of kinship rapidly developed between us.

Cries in her Sleep arrived at the Indian School without a single word of English. Within two months, she was totally fluent. Nor did her learning how to read require much more time than that. Before her first year had passed, she began devouring books at an unbelievable rate. By the time she was thirteen years old, she claimed to have read every book in the school library (some ten thousand volumes, by my estimate). She is the only certifiable genius I have ever known.

"After we graduate," she suggested to me, "let's go live in Paris and become artists like Mary Cassatt and Berthe Morisot."

"And do what for money?" I asked. "We can't count on selling the pictures we paint. It takes decades for the public to begin to appreciate any new artist."

She just shrugged, as though money matters were so trivial as not to merit consideration.

"Listen," I told her. "I don't want to starve, and I categorically refuse to steal."

"Well, then you'll simply have to marry a banker or an industrialist or perhaps a railroad tycoon. Then, you can hire me to be your travel companion or your lady's maid."

The only men to whom I, at that that age, was attracted were strapping big footballers or handsome young musicians. The idea of marrying some dull middle-aged businessman was absolutely repulsive to me.

"No, thanks," I said. "Why don't *you* marry a banker and hire *me* to be *your* travel companion?"

Cries in her Sleep shook her head emphatically. "That would never do. You're the one with the looks. And anyway, marriage is not in the cards for me. I'm much too independent. No man would put up with me. But I think marriage might suit you quite well. You have the temperament for it. Just pick somebody rich."

"Humpf!" was all I could think to say.

The next time Cries in her Sleep brought up the subject of our becoming artists and going abroad, she actually suggested that we could pay our way by "selling our bodies." Other than rolling my eyes, I did not respond. I knew that she was not serious. She was just being provocative.

"I wonder why people describe prostitution that way," she mused. "One does not actually sell one's body, you know; it's more like a short-term lease."

I had to laugh at that.

Years later, when we eventually did make our way to Paris and were forced to give serious consider to prostitution as a means of survival, we privately referred to the oldest profession as "the real-estate business."

In 1904, Cries in her Sleep and I, along with several other "exemplary scholars" of the Carlisle Indian Industrial School, traveled by train to St Louis to attend the Louisiana Purchase Exposition (popularly known as the *St Louis World's Fair*). There we tasted pizza for the first time (two cents per slice), sat in on lectures by Lakota Chiefs Red Cloud and Blue Horse, and attended a concert that featured the Haskell Indian Band. Oh, there were countless other attractions as well, but these, for us, were the highlights of the fair.

Late the following winter, the Carlisle Indian Industrial School welcomed a party of six former war chiefs of great repute: American Horse, Quanah Parker, Geronimo, Buckskin Charlie, Little Plume, and Hollow Horn Bear. The aged warriors were led on a walking tour of the school grounds, lecture halls, class rooms, band stand, art studio, and industrial shops. American Horse was especially keen to see everything, for his own sons Ben and Samuel had attended this same school a few years earlier.

Of the six leaders, only Geronimo seemed bored and unimpressed. I did not much like him. Cries in her Sleep said of him, "He's not a man I'd buy a horse from. He seems shifty to me."

The six war chiefs were on their way to Washington City, to participate in the inaugural parade of President Theodore Roosevelt. The Carlisle Indian Industrial School's forty-six-piece brass band and cadet rifle corps, three hundred fifty strong, were also to participate. A dress rehearsal was, therefore, staged down the main street of the town of Carlisle. It was spectacular. The six chiefs, in full battle regalia with painted faces and feathered headdresses, led the procession on horseback. The band came next and then the smartly uniformed cadet corps.

How I wished that I might travel to the nation's capital and witness the actual event on the fourth of March! Unfortunately, I was not to be there, but Cries in her Sleep received a last-minute invitation from the school's trustees. Besides those actually marching in the parade, only a handful of Carlisle Indian students would be in attendance as spectators.

"Oh, Sky Eyes," Cries in her Sleep told me afterward, "you can't begin to know how beautiful and how exciting it all was. I wish you could have been there with me."

"Tell me all about it."

"There must have been a hundred different bands from colleges and universities all over the country, uniforms in every style and color imaginable, precision drill teams from the army, navy, and marines, but the Indians stole the show. When those mounted chiefs in their war bonnets appeared before the presidential box, Mr Roosevelt waved his hat vigorously at them, and then he and his entire party rose to their feet in salute and remained standing until our band and cadet corps had passed. It was the only time he stood up during the entire parade. I'll tell you, Sky Eyes,

I have never been more proud. I'd die for that man."

That same year, 1905, one of our campus periodicals, *The Carlisle Arrow*, published an astonishingly enlightened article by Commissioner of Indian Affairs Francis E Leupp. That article included the following passage:

> It seems to me that one of the errors good people fall into in dealing with the Indian is taking it for granted that their first duty is to make a White man out of him.... The Indian is a natural warrior, a natural logician, a natural artist. We have room for all three in our highly organized social system. Let us not make the mistake, in the process, of absorbing them, of washing out of them whatever is distinctly Indian.

Commissioner Leupp then recruited Native American artist Angel De Cora to expand the arts program at Carlisle and authorized her to offer instruction in traditional Native American arts and crafts, including basketry, weaving, leatherwork, ceramics, beadwork, jewelry, and ledger art. Students pitched in to help with construction of a new art studio and gallery just inside the main gate of the campus. That building was completed in 1907, the year of my graduation.

I immediately applied for and was awarded an assistant teaching position under Miss De Cora. Because I was particularly adept at painting and drawing, I was allowed to teach those two subjects pretty much on my own. My star pupil, of course, was Cries in her Sleep, who soon surpassed me in her ability to render lifelike portraits of her fellow students.

It was about this time that I began to be courted by a young journalist named *Clovis Oliphant,* whom I first met whilst he was on campus conducting interviews with art students and making photographs of them at work in our new facility. Not only did Clovis write beautifully, he was a first-rate photographer as well. I was so bewitched by his cleverness and his good looks that he could have asked anything of me and I should have been powerless to deny him.

Nor, apparently, was I the only person impressed with his talent. *The Washington Post* soon made him a generous offer of employment. He gave notice at *The Sentinel* and elicited from me a promise to write him long letters every week.

"But only if you're going to write me back," I amended.

"Oh, I shall. And we can still see each other from time to time. Only a hundred or so miles will separate us. That's nothing really."

I sighed. "A hundred or so miles seems very far indeed. Only once in my entire life have I ventured any further from this school than Harrisburg."

"You're a swell girl, Brenda. I'm going to miss you terribly."

"I'm already missing you, Clovis. Just thinking about your being so far away makes me feel lonely."

He held my face lightly in both his hands and gazed adoringly into my eyes. I thought for sure that he was about declare his undying love for me, but instead, he merely said, "I really do like you a lot, Brenda."

"I like you too, Clovis."

Then he kissed me, and I knew without a doubt that I was desperately in love. I wanted more than anything to tell him how I felt. But what kind of girl would that have made me? Propriety, that cruel tyrant, dictates that a man must always be the first to reveal his heart.

CHAPTER 2

THE NEW STATE OF OKLAHOMA

On the sixteenth of November, 1907, Indian Territory, Cimarron Territory (formerly known as *No Man's Land*), and Oklahoma Territory were merged to create what now became the forty-sixth state of the United States: Oklahoma. Insomuch as Cries in her Sleep's family farm was in Oklahoma Territory and under protection of the Kiowa, Wichita, and Caddo Agency, this was a matter of some importance to her, as well as to students of the Choctaw, Sac and Fox, Towaconie (Tawakoni), Muscogee Creek, and Comanche tribes.

Of course, most nations represented at the Carlisle School had no connection whatsoever to the new state of Oklahoma. These included the Sioux, Cheyenne, Oneida, Pueblo, Hopi, Navajo, Modoc, Mohave, Chippewa, Alaskan, Nez Perce, Blackfoot, Coeur d' Alene, Zuni, Ute, Iroquois, Mohawk, and many more.

In any event, it was whilst Cries in her Sleep was embroiled in a heated debate as to whether Oklahoma statehood was a good thing or bad that an urgent telegraph arrived advising her that her mother was gravely ill and not expected to survive much longer.

"I have to go to her," she told me. "Will you come too? I really don't want to go alone."

"Of course," I said. "I can be packed in an hour." What else does one say to one's best friend?

I did not yet own a suitcase or a trunk, but I did have a large picnic hamper with a hinged top. Clovis had bought it for us to take picnic lunches into the countryside. Of the clothes I decided to take, those that would not fit into the basket, I placed in a pillow case, which I then tied securely with a blue hair ribbon. Cries in her Sleep improvised similarly, and we were on our way, Chaplain Vance graciously agreeing to drive us to the nearest train station in his roomy new Clark automobile, of which he was inordinately proud. As we departed the school, a kitchen worker rushed out to hand us each a sack lunch to take with us.

"Thank you," we said in unison and waved our goodbyes to all that came out to see us off.

We were able to make the greatest part of the journey by rail in relative comfort. The next thirty miles or so by Concord coach is not an experience I ever hope to repeat, but the final ten-miles in an open buckboard was even worse. There is no way to adequately describe the torture of that bumpy, dusty ride. In the East, where major highways had long since been MacAdamized, stage lines now employed motor coaches, but in the West, where few roads were yet paved, horse-drawn transportation was still widely depended upon.

The home to which Cries in her Sleep returned was a hovel so wretched that it breaks my heart to think that any human beings in the world should have no better place to lay their heads than that. It was all I could do to conceal my horror at the desperate situation I found my friend's family struggling with. Oh, god! The hopelessness in all their eyes haunts me still.

I believe that Cries in her Sleep's mother had clung fiercely to life days after her allotted time on earth was up, determined to see her daughter's face one last time. And once she had done so, she smiled her satisfaction and passed peacefully into the next world. The burial, which was carried out within a few hours, was attended by a score of neighbors, all of whom brought food to share with the grieving family. An ancient and decrepit shaman showed up to recite a brief graveside chant.

Decency required that we not take our leave too hastily. And yet, we were both anxious to be anywhere else in the world. It was pure grace that kept us there another entire week, meeting people, shaking hands, nodding and smiling at their anecdotes, and just being folksy. Finally, we were on our way back to Pennsylvania.

At the town where we were to transfer from the horse-drawn stage coach to the railroad, we faced a five-hour wait for our train. In the station, we fell into conversation with an Indian lady so bent and wrinkled that she must have been at least a hundred years old. In the course of our chat, she happened to mention that she was of the Choctaw Nation. I immediately fell to my knees and began kissing her feet and thanking her.

"Here, here, child," she said. "What is this in aid of?"

With tears in my eyes, I looked up into her ancient face. "I am Irish. I owe you my life, as do thousands of my countrymen. The generosity of the Choctaw people during the potato famine is something no Irishman will ever forget."

The old lady pulled me up and sat me beside her and wrapped her arm around my shoulder. "You are not old enough to remember those terrible days. I can barely recall them myself."

"My ma told me. Every night, when she tucked me into bed, she would tell me that story. She did not mean for me ever to forget."

There were, of course, Choctaw children at the Carlisle School, but they knew nothing about the starvation that Ireland had faced between 1845 and 1849. Nor were they aware that their ancestors, only a few short years after enduring the Trail of Tears themselves, had contributed an astonishing sum toward a relief fund. This lady was clearly old enough to have participated in raising that money. I offered her my dearest treasure, a cameo ring inherited from my mother.

"It is the only thing of value that I own," I told her. "I want you to have it."

"I shall treasure it always, for I know that it is a gift from the heart. You are a good girl, Sky Eyes. Your parents must be very proud of you."

When, finally, we were on our way again in the relative comfort of a Pullman car, Cries in her Sleep laid her head in my lap and said, "I hope you can take me with you when you move."

Clovis and I were now formally engaged to be married, you see, our plan being to live in New York City. Clovis's employment at the *Washington Post* had lasted but a few months. A difference of editorial opinion with his supervisor had led to his angry resignation. Happily, he had immediately secured an even better position at *Collier's*. I meant to finish the school year at Carlisle before joining Clovis in New York City. Chaplain Vance had wanted to perform a wedding service for us in Carlisle, Pennsylvania, at the chapel on the campus of Dickinson College, but Clovis and I had decided instead on a civil ceremony in Manhattan.

Mind you, I could no more imagine my life without Cries in her Sleep than could she imagine hers without me. We seemed to be soul twins.

"Of course I'm taking you with me." I said. "You can't really believe that I'd ever leave you behind."

"Aren't you concerned in the least that Clovis might object?"

"He'd better not. Anyway, why would he?"

"I don't know. He might. Don't you think you should ask him before agreeing to take me with you?"

"No," I said firmly. "The way it works with Clovis and me is that I tell him what I want, and he immediately moves heaven and earth to make it so. I shouldn't have it any other way, and neither, apparently, would he. He worships the ground I walk on, you know."

Cries in her Sleep laughed. "Lucky you! And lucky me as well, I suppose! I pray we never tax his generosity of spirit."

CHAPTER 3

GREENWICH VILLAGE

Clovis was indeed as amenable to Cries in her Sleep's living with us as I had promised he would be. He always referred to her, by the way, as his "sister-in-law." In order to be able to afford a private room for her, however, we were forced to look at apartments in neighborhoods that Clovis might otherwise have been not inclined to consider.

Cries in her Sleep and I were thrilled beyond words when Clovis finally consented to our renting a small three-room apartment above a taproom in Greenwich Village. That traditionally Italian and Irish Catholic neighborhood was just beginning to acquire a reputation as a haven for artists, writers, fanatical do-gooders, radical intellectuals, and non-conformists of every stripe. This was less than a decade before John Sloan, Marcel Duchamp, and a few others (drunk, no doubt) would climb to the top of Washington Square Arch in the wee hours of an icy cold winter morning to loudly announce Greenwich Village's secession from the United States.

In any event, Cries in her Sleep and I immediately set about to insinuate ourselves into the bohemian community of the Village, and I made a point always to introduce myself by my maiden name. Please understand, I was not pretending to be single. I had no desire to deny my wedded status. But I had long been signing my artwork *Brenda Murphy*, and I was loathe to change my signature. What small following I had I did not wish to lose. To Clovis's work friends, of course, I was *Mrs Oliphant* and delighted to be so known.

Cries in her Sleep, on our very first visit to an art show at an underground coffee house, introduced herself by her legal name. Taking the hint, I made a point thenceforth to refer to her as *Dolores Hummingbird*. Only in private did I still address her as *Cries in her Sleep*. And only in private now did she call me *Sky Eyes*.

Of the two of us, I was the first to sell a painting—a portrait of Dolores in traditional Native American dress—but before I could make my next sale, Dolores sold seven paintings in rapid succession: all New York street scenes. Not only was she a lot more successful than I at turning her talent into lucre, she was, I have to admit, a much better artist than I was. She made money too (though never a lot) by sitting for other artists. Next to the notorious Evelyn Nesbit, obsession with whom had, two years earlier, led to a murder, Dolores was probably the most sought-after artists' model in New York City.

I too was asked from time to time to pose nude for one or another of our Village friends, but out of concern for how my doing so might impact Clovis's career, I always declined with sincerest apologies. In any event, Dolores and I were easily accepted into the Greenwich Village circle of artists and writers.

Clovis, on the other hand, worked such long hours that, for many weeks, he simply could not find time to join us at tearooms, coffee houses, art studios, book shops, or galleries. He was eager to become acquainted with our new friends, but demands of the magazine always came first. I worried too that his starched-collar conservative style of dressing might somehow put off those poets, painters, and activists, most of whom tended to be extremely casual in their own appearance and sometimes even a bit neglectful of personal hygiene.

I need not have been concerned. When it was learned that my husband was the well-known photographer and journalist Clovis Oliphant, our new friends flocked to our apartment and clambered to meet him. Clovis might not look the part, but he was one of them: a true artist, a deep thinker, and a man of keen conscience and progressive values. He was highly respected, and I was ever so proud of him.

Though Clovis's connections at *Collier's,* Dolores and I were introduced to Gertrude Käsebier, whose photographic portraits of Iron Tail, Flying Hawk, and other Sioux notables in the 1890s had made her famous. Then through Mrs

Käsebier, we met Frances Frances Benjamin Johnston, with whose work we were already familiar, for she had, a few years earlier, visited the Carlisle Indian School in order to make photographs there.

With those two ladies as our guides, Dolores and I visited the Little Galleries of the Photo-Secession at 291 Fifth Avenue. Later that very year (1908), this establishment, operated by Alfred Stieglitz and Edward Steichen, would be renamed simply *291* and would begin exhibiting non-photographic works as well, works by Pablo Picasso, for instance, Henri Matisse, Henri Rousseau, Paul Cézanne, Constantin Brâncuși, Auguste Rodin, Francis Picabia, and Marcel Duchamp. Today, however, the images we viewed were all photographic, many by Stieglitz and Steichen themselves, others by Mrs Käsebier, Alvin Langdon Coburn, and Clarence White. As you might expect, we were absolutely enchanted.

Had I not so much invested in paints and brushes and had I not already one photographer in my household, I think I might have been tempted to become a photographer myself. As an artistic medium, photography has a magical appeal. At least, to me it does.

In any event, Dolores and I pooled our money and bought two prints that day: a portrait of Evelyn Nesbit by Mrs Käsebier and an image of two young women kissing by Clarence White. With Clovis's blessing we hung them both in the large middle room of our apartment.

This middle room served as our breakfast room, dining room, and parlor. It was through this room that one entered our apartment. At the far end of the room was a shabby little kitchen area. A dining table with eight chairs, all showing much wear, dominated the rest of the room. A door to the right communicated with Dolores's tiny bedroom. Another door to the left opened into the somewhat-larger bedroom shared by Clovis and me. And finally, on the back wall between the ice box and the rust-stained kitchen sink was the door to the bathroom, which was so awful that I should not begin to know how to describe it.

Certainly, there was nothing luxurious about this apartment. In summer it was unbearably hot, and in winter, we nearly froze to death. Then too, the constant bickering of our neighbors above and to either side, not to mention the din from the Irish pub below, drove us nearly mad at times. However, despite all these nuisances, we were, for the most part, quite content there. After all, we did enjoy the benefit of hot and cold running water. Not all New Yorkers could say as much.

Most mornings, I saw Clovis off to work before full daylight. Dolores, who could have remained abed until a decent hour, made a point always to join us for breakfast. Either she would perk the coffee and make toast whilst I prepared eggs and bacon or else we might switch chores. In any case, she and I worked well together. Never once in that tiny kitchen space did we collide or get in each other's way. Nor did any of the three of us ever grate on one another's nerves, as people living in such close proximity often do.

On Sundays, of course, we allowed poor Clovis, as sleep-deprived and overworked as he was, to sleep in until almost noon. As soon as we heard him begin to stir, Dolores would prepare a tray for me to take in for him: buttered toast, marmalade, coffee, and the Sunday newspapers, which, by this time, Dolores and I should already have read and discussed at length.

For hard news, we depended primarily on the *New York Times*, and for entertainment news, we subscribed to *Variety* and also to the *Morning Tele-*

graph. Clovis was especially fond of Bat Masterson's thrice-weekly sports column in the *Telegraph*.

"Oh, my god! Stop right where you are. Don't move. I have to capture this on film."

With Clovis's tray in my hands I was standing at the side of the bed with the morning sun pouring through the windows behind me. Apparently, my husband meant to take my photograph before addressing his breakfast.

"But Clovis" I objected, "your coffee will get cold, and anyway, I'm not even dressed, and my hair's a mess."

Please do not imagine that I was naked. I was in my nightclothes, over which I was wearing a peignoir. My modesty was hardly at stake, or so I believed.

Clovis had by this time sprung out of bed on the opposite side and was now attaching a newly acquired Kodak camera to a tripod. His usual preference was for a cumbersome oversize view camera, but this morning, it seemed, he meant to put this little roll-film camera to the test.

The resulting image, which I only saw two days later, was astonishingly beautiful. It was every bit as memorable as any photograph ever published in *Camera Work* magazine or exhibited at the Little Galleries. But mercy! I might as well have been completely bare. The light behind me made my garments so gauzy in appearance that every detail of my physical person was fully revealed.

"Clovis!" I gasped, blushing to my toes. "Who has seen this?"

"No one yet," he laughed. "Would you really be embarrassed for people to see it?"

"I guess not," I said shyly. "I mean, if you wouldn't mind. Do you want to show it?"

"It's the best thing I've ever done."

"Then of course you must show it. Or publish it. Whatever you want to do with it is fine by me. I'm terribly flattered to be associate with such a masterpiece. You're a true artist, Clovis."

And so my likeness joined the two photographs by Clarence White and Gertrude Käsebier on the wall of our middle room. Visitors to our apartment never failed to admire it. Clovis even managed to sell a copy to one wealthy collector on Long Island. Not surprisingly, I began to get renewed invitations to pose for other artists and photographers in the Village.

Dolores urged me to accept. "If Clovis is willing to have you seen in such an immodest state, then he can hardly object to your posing for other artists as well."

I was not so sure. Men can be entirely unreasonable at times, and the last thing in the world I wanted to do was risk losing Clovis's affection. Finally, I simply asked him how he might feel about my sitting for some of our artist friends.

"Have you been asked?" He seemed quite surprised, which fact might have hurt my feelings somewhat had I allowed it to.

"Many times," I told him. "I've always turned them down, worried that I might cost you your job. Anyway, I shouldn't ever want to disappoint you in any way."

"Oh, my darling, how could you ever disappoint me? Don't you know how much I adore you? As for my job, it is quite secure. Of that you can be sure. They can't get along without me. So would you like to pose for these artist who have asked you?"

I nodded. "I think so. Yes, I should. Dolores does it all the time, you know, and gets paid for it too. She says that collaborating with an artist that way makes her feel like a full partner in the creative process. That's how posing for you made me feel. I like that feeling a lot, Clovis."

"Then go for it. You have my blessing. I shall never stand between you and anything you want to do."

I threw my arms around his neck and covered his face with kisses. Posing for other artists and photographers did not mean all that much to me, but Clovis's unqualified support meant everything. He was an exceptional husband, one in a million, and I fully appreciated that fact.

CHAPTER 4

CHINATOWN

Dolores and I have always had similar styles of painting, but completely different approaches. That is to say, we tend to choose different subject matter. Dolores has the amazing ability to see something extraordinary in the mundane. She paints the very scenes one observes every day, and yet her paintings all possess a magical quality that makes them very appealing. I, on the other hand, make a point to seek out the exotic. During the time we lived in Greenwich Village, most of my paintings were of nearby Chinatown and its denizens. And yet, none of my paintings were as interesting as any done by Dolores.

"What's wrong with me?" I asked in frustration, putting down my brush to pour myself a cup of coffee. "Why can't I do what you do?"

"Your paintings are really good," Dolores assured me. "I like what you do. But maybe they could be improved upon a tiny bit." She got up and moved to stand directly in front of my easel. "A little dab of white, a squiggle of red, an accent of blue-black, and this would be a work of sheer genius."

"Show me," I demanded.

She started pointing out the additions she thought I ought to make, but I could not see clearly what she meant for me to do.

"Do it for me," I begged.

"You want me to put paint to your picture?" she asked. "Are you sure?"

"I'm sure. I've done everything I know how to do. If you can turn this into something I can sell, I'll be ever so grateful."

"Oh, you could sell it now," she said, "and easily. On the other hand, a few touch-ups at just the right places could transform this into a masterpiece."

I did not really believe what she was telling me, but I urged her, nonetheless, to demonstrate.

She picked up my brush, hesitated only a moment, studying my painting, then deftly applied a few quick brushstrokes. The result was amazing.

My mouth fell open. "How did you do that? I mean, how did you know what needed to be done?"

Dolores laughed. "I don't know. I could just see what was missing. I don't know how."

"When I sign this, I want you to sign it too."

Dolores shook her head firmly. "It's your painting. The little bit of help I gave you didn't amount to much."

"I cannot take all the credit for this. Without your contribution, I should not even have had the nerve to exhibit it."

Dolores continued to protest, but eventually she gave in and added her name to the bottom left of the painting just below my own name. Then, at my urging, she worked similar miracles on all my older works, which suddenly became very popular. Nor have I ever again signed any painting that Dolores has not also signed. She, of course, does many painting entirely on her own.

Whenever either of us sold a painting, we celebrated by dining out at Delmonico's in Chinatown. Clovis with Dolores on one arm and me on the other always took a lot of teasing about his two wives.

"Oh, my goodness, no!" Clovis would say. "One wife is all I can handle. This other one is my sister-in-law. Why don't you marry her and take her off my hands?"

Another favorite place of ours in Chinatown was the Pelham Café, which boasted the most-amusing singing waiter. A young Jewish fellow about my own age served us drinks and made up new and very naughty lyrics to popular songs. His name was *Israel*. We quite adored him.

Ragtime was the music of the bohemian community in those days, and no one was a more-enthusiastic fan than I was. In observance of my nineteenth birthday, Clovis bought me a new Grafonola, thus contributing to our little apartment's becoming one of the primary gathering places for artist and intellectuals in the Village. And everyone who came brought recorded music for us to play.

The Grafonola, by the way, was introduced by Columbia in 1907. It was revolutionary in that it had no external horn, as did the Disc Graphophone, which it replaced. Mind you, the

Grafonola did, in fact, have a horn, but that horn was internal and not apparent.

Amongst those that now became regular visitors to our little apartment were Robert Henri, John French Sloan, and Sloan's wife Dolly. Clovis, incidentally, was already well acquainted with Sloan through *Collier's*. Mind you, Sloan was not employed by the magazine, but he did frequently contribute free-lance illustrations. His paintings were very much like those by Dolores: ordinary street scenes. His age at that time was thirty-seven years. His wife was five years younger.

Dolly worked in a department store by day and devoted much of her free time to campaigning for women's suffrage and other issues dear to her heart. I am not sure, but I believe that she was a member of the Socialist Party. Certainly, she was very sympathetic to their cause and participated in their marches and demonstrations, carrying placards and handing out leaflets. Even so, she was miserably unhappy and drank too much, causing her husband no end of concern, for he loved his wife in much the same way that Clovis loved me. Somehow, Dolly, who, by the way, was well-read, intelligent, and quite pretty, could never feel secure in Sloan's devotion to her, even though it was abundantly clear to everyone else.

"He is so far above me," she confided to me one night. "I live in dread of the day it dawns on him how unworthy I am. It is inevitable that he will leave me, you know."

I myself never posed for Sloan. Dolores did, but only once, I believe. On those rare occasions that Sloan elected to do figurative work, his wife was his preferred model. Dolly must have been unavailable the day he asked Dolores to sit for him.

One curious habit of Sloan's that I recall most vividly was his assiduity in keeping a diary. It seems to me as though he must have written in it almost every day. Most assuredly, it filled up very rapidly.

Sloan's good friend Robert Henri, a successful portraitist, was forty-three years old when he first began visiting our apartment. Dolores at age seventeen and I at age nineteen each sat for him a number of times. He then took it upon himself to offer us instructive criticism of our artworks. We were both extremely gratified that such an accomplished artist would take us seriously enough to wish to become our mentor. Nor were we two the only young female artists with whom he surrounded himself. There were at least half a dozen others, none without a great deal of talent. We were in good company, and we knew it.

That same year, the Macbeth Gallery, owned by William Macbeth, hosted a group exhibition for eight artists, including Robert Henri and John French Sloan. The other six were known to Dolores, Clovis, and me as well, but we were not particularly close to any of them. Their names are *William Glackens, George Luks, Everett Shinn, Arthur Bowen Davies, Ernest Lawson*, and *Maurice Prendergast*. Such an impression did this show make on art critics and the public alike that the eight artists represented have come to be known collectively as the *Eight*. Incidentally, five of the Eight (not Prendergast, Lawson, or Davies) are also associated with the so-called *Ashcan School*.

Dolores, Clovis and I attended that show together. It was there that we were first introduced to George Bellows, who has since come to be widely regarded as the greatest American artist ever. He was a former protégé of Robert Henri. Also present at that show were authors Edith Wharton and Willa Cather and photojournalist Jessie Tarbox Beal, whom Dolores and I had met in 1904 at the Louisiana Purchase Exposition. In fact, she had taken our picture there.

CHAPTER 5

ALEXANDER'S RAGTIME BAND

On the sixth of May, 1910, King Edward VII died, and Clovis promptly took ship for England in hopes of arriving in time for the state funeral on the twentieth. This was an unparalleled photographic opportunity. It was assumed that heads of state of many nations would be in attendance. Dolores and I should very much have liked to accompany Clovis, but arrangements simply could not be made in time. In fact, the only available berth for Clovis was a cabin shared with three other journalists.

That same year, Eduard Käsebier died. He was the husband of photographer Gertrude Käsebier. Dolores and I attended the funeral. Mrs Käsebier, we noticed, seemed to be having extreme difficulty controlling her emotions.

"I wonder whether she was trying not to cry or trying not to laugh," Dolores said to me on our way home afterward. "I don't believe for a minute that she loved that man."

"Maybe once, she did," I suggested, "but in the end, she didn't even like him very much, or so it seemed to me. I wonder how a marriage can go so wrong."

"At least, you don't have to worry about that. Your husband is an absolute jewel, and he cherishes you."

"I know," I said. "I'm very lucky."

Clovis did not immediately return to New York after the king's funeral. He was meeting lots of interesting people, he wrote, and taking "mountains of marvelous photographs." Nor did he invite Dolores and me to join him in England. He simply had not made up his mind how long he intended to stay. Quite possibly, he might abide there until after the coronation of King George V.

And when might that be? I queried him by cable.

The date, it seemed, had not been set, but it would be after "an appropriate period of mourning."

And so for many months, Dolores and I were on our own in New York. We developed an entirely new routine that did not revolve around Clovis's work schedule. Even though I missed Clovis desperately, I had to admit that I quite liked my new-found independence. Indeed, I actually began to dread having to give it up someday.

Because Dolores and I often stayed out now until all hours of the night, we tended to sleep in until almost noon. And because I missed feeling Clovis's body next to mine in the bed at night, I invited Dolores to take his place.

"I love sleeping with you," she whispered as she snuggled up against my body. "It reminds me of when we were little and you used to lie beside me in my bed and hold me until I drifted off."

"I like it too," I murmured, kissing her goodnight.

"I know it's a wicked thing to say," she added, "but I wish Clovis would stay in England so you and I could be together like this forever."

"Shh!" I warned her. "Don't say things like that, Cries in her Sleep. I love you with all my heart, but there will always be a place in my life for Clovis."

"I know. I was just being silly. Don't be upset with me, please."

I reassured her with another kiss. "I'm not upset with you, my darling girl. Now go to sleep."

Clovis's next letter advised me that he had quit his job with *Collier's* to work on a strictly free-lance basis. In the short term, he warned, our income might take a bit of a hit, but before very long, he would be earning even more than he had been paid by the magazine. At least, that was his hope.

The rest of his letter was filled with amusing anecdotes about his new friends, George Merrill and Edward Carpenter, a homosexual couple living together openly in defiance of the law. Clovis was quite impressed that these two prominent gentlemen were willing to risk so much in an effort to change the prevailing attitude of intolerance for those whose lifestyle choices were somewhat unconventional.

Shortly after the first of the year (1911), a new song "Alexander's Ragtime Band" swept the country. I loved it. Dolores loved. Everyone we knew loved it. Emma Carus was the first to record it, but soon every musician in the country was offering his own version.

When Dolores read aloud to me from the *New York Telegraph* that the song's previously unknown composer, one Irving Berlin, would be performing "Alexander's Ragtime Band" at Oscar Hammerstein's Victoria Theatre, I was mad for us to attend.

"Let's get dressed then," she agreed, "and go see if there are still any tickets to be had. This is a show that's bound to sell out pretty fast."

Not only did we get tickets, we got really good seats right up front and in a row with several of our friends from the Village, many of whom, apparently, knew something that we did not. Imagine our great surprise to discover that we were already personally acquainted with the performer that stepped out onto the stage. Irving Berlin, it turned out, was none other than Israel, the singing waiter from the Pelham Café.

When the sheet music for "Alexander's Ragtime Band" had been published, the composer had been identified only as *I Berlin*. The promoters, entirely on their own and for reasons known only to themselves, decided to identify him as *Irving Berlin*, and by that name he is still known.

In any event, the theater was packed full of Israel's friends, family members, and supporters from the East Village, the West Village, Chinatown, and Chelsea. Such an enthusiastic welcome we gave him that the commencement of his performance was delayed for several minutes. Of course, he finally was allowed to play, and the critics loved him as much as the audience did. An article in the *New York Telegraph* describing Israel's warm reception included the following passage:

> All the little writer could do was to finger the buttons on his coat while tears ran down his cheeks....

CHAPTER 6
RMS Olympic

In 1911, the newly built *RMS Olympic,* pride of the White Star Line, was the largest ocean liner in the world. Her maiden voyage commenced at Southampton on the fourteenth of June. After making brief stops at Cherbourg and Queenstown (known since 1920 as *Cobh*), she sailed for New York City, arriving on the twenty-first of June. Dolores and I were amongst the throng that turned out to welcome her. And when she made her return voyage, we were onboard.

The designation *RMS*, by the way, stands for *Royal Mail Ship*. I know this because Dolores asked the ship's purser, and he informed us. He also went on to say that the *Olympic* would soon be joined in service by two identical sister ships, the *Titanic* and the *Britannic*. The former was already under construction in Belfast, and work was shortly to begin there on the latter.

"Some ship names," Dolores said brightly, "bear the prefix *SS*. I suppose that must stand for *Steam Ship*."

The purser laughed. "That would certainly make sense, miss. It was a very good guess on your part, but in fact, *SS* stands for *Single Screw*."

Dolores giggled in spite of herself, and I, to move the conversation in a safer direction, asked a question to which I already knew the answer. "And *HMS*?"

"*His Majesty's Ship*. Only ships of the Royal Navy are so designated."

I nodded. "Thank you, purser. "This has been a very informative conversation. I pray we haven't kept you too long from your duties."

"And shore facilities as well," he added.

"I beg your pardon."

"The Royal Navy identifies its shore facilities as *stone frigates,* and puts the prefix *HMS* before the names of those facilities."

"How quaint!" Dolores exclaimed, genuinely delighted with this curious tidbit of information.

Thus encouraged, the purser continued. "A variation of *HMS,* by the way, is *HBMS,* which stands for *His Britannic Majesty's Ship.* I don't believe *HBMS* is much used these day, but a hundred years ago, it certainly was. Some very famous ships were so designated."

Dolores," I said, nudging her with my elbow, "we have to go now, or we're going to miss the last seating for dinner."

"Yes, of course," she answered me. Then to the purser, she said, "Please excuse us. It's been a pleasure chatting with you, but we really do have to run."

"Certainly, miss. I hope I haven't caused you to miss your dinner."

A long apologetic letter from Clovis back in the spring had informed me that my husband's affections were no longer mine alone. Initially, I had felt wounded and angry, but as I read on—weeping, I must admit—I came to appreciate that no one should ever be blamed for unbidden feelings of attraction for another person. To give Clovis credit, he had not yet acted on his feelings for this other person, a young man he had met at the home of George Merrill and Edward Carpenter. Clovis had, so far, refused to violate our wedding vows, but had wanted us now to renegotiate those vows.

"But this is actually a good thing," Dolores had argued. "Don't you see? This gives you and me permission to finally have the kind of relationship we've always longed for."

"What the hell are you going on about?" I had screamed in her face, immediately reducing her to tears as well. "My life is in ruins, and you're talking nonsense."

She had run from my room to barricade herself in her own room. Eventually, of course, I had calmed down, taken command of my reckless emotions, and gone to Dolores, begging for her forgiveness.

"Never!" she had said fiercely.

I had pleaded with her, but she had cruelly resisted my efforts at reconciliation. Finally, I had confessed my own unnatural desire for her—a feeling for which I had always been ashamed and embarrassed—and with that admission, she had at last relented.

We had then kissed as we had never kissed before. And, oh, how hungrily had we undressed each other! How desperately had we made love for the very first time!

Clovis and I had continued to exchange letters throughout the spring. We had agreed to stay married to each other, but had decided never again to live together. I still loved Clovis, and I believed him when he swore that he still loved me. But Dolores and I had made up our minds to move to Paris, as we had always dreamed of doing. And now, we were on our way. Once we were settled there, Clovis and his new boyfriend would be more than welcome to pay us a visit.

CHAPTER 7

NATIVE AMERICAN IN PARIS

At the time of our arrival in Paris, the primary arts district—a close equivalent, in fact, to New York City's Greenwich Village—was Montmartre in the Eighteenth Arrondissement in the northern part of the city. This low-rent bohemian community had been, for decades, a Mecca for artists, who flocked there from Russia, Romania, Germany, Spain, Italy, England, America, and other places. Degas, Monet, and Renoir had moved on. Toulouse-Lautrec and Vincent van Gogh had both died, but Suzanne Valadon still painted here, as did her son Maurice Utrillo and countless newcomers whose names were just beginning to be known to the general public: Picasso, for example, Modigliani, Brâncuși, Matisse, Braque, and Dufy.

In Montmartre are located the Sacré-Cœur Basilica, the Montmartre Abbey, the Martyrium of Saint Denis, the Moulin Rouge, Le Chat Noir, the stairs of the Rue Foyatier, the Vineyard in Rue Saint-Vincent, and of course, the famous windmills. Dolores and I spent hours at each of these sites, making sketches or painting out of doors.

Le Chat Noir, which we visited at 68 Boulevard de Clichy, was not, we learned, the original cabaret of Rodolphe Salis, nor even the site to which he later moved, but merely a café with the same name established by Jehan Chargot in 1907 (ten years after Salis's death and the closing of the first Chat Noir). Still, we were thrilled beyond all imagination to be sipping aperitifs there at a tiny table for two, pretending to be a lot more sophisticated than we really were.

It was, in fact, at Le Chat Noir that we first met Suzanne Valadon. She simply walked up to our table, introduced herself, and explained that, having seen us painting out of doors on several occasions, she knew that we ourselves were artists, and she was hoping that we might be amenable to sitting for her.

"When I was your age and still trying to get my art career off the ground," she confided. "I found posing for other artists to be an agreeable way of supplementing my meager income."

"We too," I agreed.

"To sit for you, *madame,*" said Dolores, "would be such an honor that, could we afford to, we should be happy to pose for free."

The great artist found this highly amusing, but promptly assured us that she could afford to pay us well and fully intended to do so. A truly fortuitous encounter that was too; for we had been within days of having to make our first venture into the real-estate business.

Through Suzanne Valadon, we also became casually acquainted with her son, Maurice Utrillo. Of course, neither of us was ever asked to pose for him; he is, after all, exclusively a cityscape painter. Nor did we find him easy to get to know. I can tell you this much about him: he is an extreme introvert and a very heavy drinker. Still, he is a very prolific artist, and I quite adore all the pictures he produces, street scenes of Montmartre.

Crossing Place du Tertre one evening just at dusk, we were accosted by a dark-skinned street urchin of about ten years. I figured the boy to be of North African ethnicity (Arab or possibly Berber).

"Please, *mademoiselle,*" he said to me. "You are the American ladies, yes?"

I assented, and he urged us to follow him. "*Monsieur* wishes to see you. Come quick."

I tried to question the boy, but he had very little French and no English whatsoever. It did occur to us to be wary, but curiosity soon got the better of us. We followed our guide a short distance to a ramshackle building at 13 Rue Ravignan. The boy entered, and after a moment's hesitation, we did likewise.

The inside of what seemed to be a vast warehouse or former factory had been crudely subdivided to create a score of quite large but primitive art studios. Motioning for us to come along after him, the boy entered one of these studios, where several men and about half as many women were standing around talking and drinking wine in a number of small groups. Music could be heard above the babble of conversation, but the source was not immediately apparent.

The boy tugged on the sleeve of one of the men. "The American ladies, sir, I bring them, like you say."

Without even glancing around, the man, who was pontificating loudly on the purpose and value of art, reached into his pocket for a coin, which he then passed to the child, who now departed the premises. An attractive young women extricated herself from one of the groups to bring Dolores and me each a glass of dark red wine.

"I'm Fernande," she said. "Make yourselves at home. He'll be with you shortly."

We still had no idea who "he" was nor why he had summoned us. We sipped the wine and perused the thirty or so paintings that hung on the walls of the studio. Most, if not all, I felt, were extremely amateurish, not well executed by any means. Lest we be overheard, however, I refrained from expressing my opinion aloud to Dolores. We could discuss this later in private.

Shortly, we were joined by our host, who, without bothering to introduce himself, welcomed us to his studio and asked us our names.

We told him, and yet, he still neglected to tell us his. We later came to realize that, in his great arrogance, he assumed that we knew who he was.

"How did you find this place?" he asked. "We rarely get foreign visitors."

"But, *monsieur,*" Dolores objected, "you sent for us. The Arab boy told us to come."

The man laughed uproariously. "I am so sorry! A case of mistaken identity. I sent him for two other ladies. But I am glad you are here, all the same. There are never enough ladies at these gatherings. Stick around if you like. You might meet someone fascinating. Do you, by any chance, have a particular interest in art?"

"We both paint," Dolores said. "We were trained by Robert Henri."

"Also," I added, "we are models. Recently, we have been sitting for Suzanne Valadon. Perhaps, there are other artists here who would like to hire us as well. We need the work."

"Then you are especially welcome. I have no doubt that you will find employment as models this very night. Come. Let me introduce you to everyone."

Our host, we soon realized, was Pablo Picasso, whose rise to fame had only just begun. Oddly, it seemed to me, his friends always addressed him simply as *Picasso.* I do not believe I ever heard anyone call him by his given name. Nor is *Picasso* even his own legal surname, but his mother's maiden name. Picasso's actual surname is *Ruiz.* Why he chooses not to use that name is anyone's guess. Dolores has speculated that he uses his mother's name so as she told me herself. Her own sexuality would not be awakened fully until the 1920s, by which time, many in the Arts community would have come to hail her as the *Queen of Montparnasse*.

A similar royal title, *Queen of Bohemia,* was one day soon to be bestowed upon Nina Hamnett, but let me tell you first about Nina's initial encounter with Amedeo Modigliani on her first full day in Montparnasse. If you have already heard this story, I apologize. I shall be as brief as possible, but I dare not skip over it completely, for there are surely some readers to whom this will be new.

Dolores, of course, wanted Nina to rent a studio at la Ruche, but Nina insisted first on seeing what other studios might be available in the neighborhood. She spent the entire day looking at one property after another, eventually deciding that she could not do better than la Ruche. For dinner, she stopped at Café de la Rotonde. The man at the next table, she noticed, kept staring at her.

She smiled and nodded at him, and that was all the encouragement he needed. He rose to his feet, stepped closer, and introduced himself, "Modigliani, painter and Jew."

It was Victor Libion the restaurateur that first told me this story. But I heard it also from Dolores, who had it directly from Nina.

In any event, Nina rented a studio at la Ruche and immediately began a passionate affair with Modigliani, her romantic interest in Dolores apparently forgotten. Nina, it seems, is one of those women who are only capable of being enamored of one person at time; although her romantic interest in anyone is extraordinarily short lived.

Dolores, of course, was crushed to be so casually dropped. I felt sorry for her, but dared not commiserate with her or even take notice of her unhappiness, lest it seem to her that I were gloating. I went about my business as though nothing were amiss, and Dolores recovered in short order.

Within a few weeks, Nina had dumped Modigliani as well, to marry Norwegian artist Edgar de Bergen, who would one day soon change his name to *Roald Kristian*. As far as I know, Nina and Roald (or Edgar) are still legally married, but she hasn't lived with him in ages. She has carried on affairs with countless men and women, including Roger Fry, whose interest in her she had assiduously ignored back in 1911. Walter Sickert took her on as his protégé, and she may or may not have had an affair with him. She certainly spent a lot of time in his company. She posed for various painters and sculptors, and once in a café, she stripped off all her clothes to dance naked on a tabletop. You can see, I think, how she came to be called the *Queen of Bohemia*. For the Omega Workshops in London, Nina designed rugs, furniture, and other decorator items.

CHAPTER 16
THE GREAT WAR

Amedeo Clemente Modigliani, with his dashing good looks, might have appeared to a casual observer to be in perfect health. The color in his cheeks and his godlike physique bespoke a robust constitution. And yet, Modigliani was afflicted with tuberculosis. As the disease progressed and symptoms became more severe, Modigliani's drinking and drugging increased, and his behavior became more and more erratic. It was not unheard of for him to become violent. Modigliani's family and closest friends had always called him *Dedo,* but within the community of artists, models, and writers of Montparnasse, he was known as *Modi,* that nick name being a clever pun on the French word *maudit,* meaning *cursed.*

In 1914, almost immediately after Modigliani's dalliance with Nina Hamnett ended, he began a more-serious love affair with the English writer Beatrice Hastings, who moved in with him at la Ruche. She would stay with him for about two years.

Born *Emily Alice Haigh* in London, Beatrice Hastings (as she was known to us in Paris) had spent much of her youth in South Africa. Immediately before coming to Montparnasse, she had worked at *The New Age*, a British literary journal, where she had regularly contributed articles written under a dozen or more different pseudonyms. Like most of the other women of our bohemian circle, Beatrice was without sexual preference. She was as susceptible to falling in love with another of her own gender as with someone of the opposite gender. She was an obsessive lover, not by any means promiscuous. Her affairs might not last as long as she wished, but whilst each endured, she remained totally faithful. Before coming to Paris, Beatrice had enjoyed romantic liaisons with AR Orage (founding editor at *The New Age*), Katherine Mansfield (a writer), and Percy Wyndham Lewis (a painter associated with Vorticism, which is akin to Cubism).

In Paris, Beatrice was a close friend to the poet Max Jacob and the adventure novelist Charles Beadle, but my sense is that neither of these two men was ever invited to share her bed. Mind you, I cannot be certain of that. I do know that she was quite close to both of them.

When Dolores and I were first introduced to her, we could honestly say that we were already somewhat familiar with her work, for we had in our possession a pamphlet written in 1909 by her under the pseudonym *Beatrice Tina* and titled "Woman's Worst Enemy: Woman." This little essay we had discussed at length between ourselves and with Miss Stein and Miss Toklas as well. But Beatrice's finest literary talent, as we were soon to discover, lay in her uncanny ability to parody other writers, including HG Wells and Ezra Pound.

In the late spring of that year (1914), Marc Chagall was offered the opportunity to exhibit some of his latest artworks in Germany. He crated them up and traveled with them. Then after consigning them to a highly respected dealer in Berlin, he traveled on to Vitebsk, where his fiancée Bella still waited for him. His intention was to marry her and promptly return with her to Paris. The outbreak of war trapped him in the Russian Empire. He and Bella would not reach France until after the armistice.

On the twenty-eighth of July, Austria-Hungary declared war on Serbia. My first thought was this would be just another of those tiresome Balkan wars. I prayed that Clovis would not feel the need to cover it, as he had the two previous ones. It certainly did not occur to me and I don't believe it occurred to anyone we knew that France and Britain would soon be drawn into the conflict.

But tensions were high; alliances had been forged, and a number of world leaders were playing the dangerous game of brinksmanship. Czar Nicolas II was fully prepared to commit the might of the armies of the Russian Empire to the defense of the Serbs. Kaiser Wilhelm II was equally steadfast in his determination for Germany to stand by Austria-Hungary. France and Britain were allied with Russia. Italy was bound by a mutual-defense treaty to Germany and Austria-Hungary.

On the second of August, the German army occupied the Grand Duchy of Luxembourg, and on the following day, declared war on France. On the fourth of August, German armies invaded Belgium. England promptly responded by declaring war on Germany. Hostilities would eventually spread as far as Africa and Asian. In 1917, the United States would also join this conflict, which has now come to be known as the *Great War.*

Guillaume Apollinaire, André Derain, Georges Braque, and many others from the bohemian community signed up for the French army. Modigliani—either in a passion of patriotism for his chosen country or in fear of being deported or interned should his native Italy declare war on France—attempted to enlist, but could not pass the requisite physical exam.

Italy, after waffling for several months, would indeed join the war, but on the side of Triple Entente (Russia, England, and France). Italy, Germany, and Austria-Hungary had formed the Triple Alliance. But Italy's government took the position that, while Italy was bound by treaty to defend Germany and Austria-Hungary from attack, it was not obligated to support them in aggression. What was left of the Triple Alliance would then come to be known as the *Central Powers.* Italy and the Triple Entente then became known as the *Allied Powers.* The Ottoman Empire, no doubt hoping to regain more of its lost European territory, joined the war in the side of the Central Powers. Bulgaria too sided with the Central Powers. Greece supported the Allied Powers, as did Japan.

At the very outset of the war, Dolores and I volunteered to work for the Union des Femmes de France, an equivalent organization to the Red Cross. We folded sheets; we packaged gauze bandages; we even learned how to drive a monstrous big Latil truck in order to deliver supplies to hospitals. In short, we did whatever we were called upon to do. In 1916, Miss Stein and Miss Toklas would, likewise, volunteer to drive a truck, but for the American Fund for French Wounded, rather than for the Union des Femmes de France. These two ladies would even acquire their own vehicle, a persnickety little Ford shipped over from America. They would call it *Auntie* after Miss Stein's Aunt Pauline, "who always behaved admirably in emergencies and behaved fairly well most times if she was flattered."

Dolores and I did not name the truck we drove, but then again, it did not belong to us, and whenever we were not driving it, someone else was.

CHAPTER 17

JIZZ, JAZZ, JAS, AND BLUES

Recordings of the latest American songs, even with this war going on, found their way across the Atlantic more often than you might imagine. Dolores and I, who were very keen on pop music, found it interesting to observe that ragtime was evolving in two different directions simultaneously, becoming two entirely new forms of music: jazz and blues. Nor were we the only ones to notice this trend. One music critic suggested that "Alexander's Ragtime Band" should have been called "Alexander's Jazz Band." Jazz, you see, is more complex and more sophisticated than traditional ragtime, which is usually performed by a single pianist. Of course, even with ragtime, the two hands are playing different parts. But Jazz requires a group of musicians, the parts almost always numbering more than two.

Besides "Alexander's Ragtime Band," we now added to our collection of recordings "Ballin' the Jack" performed by Prince's Band and "Memphis Blues" by WC Handy, who would eventually be regarded as the *Father of Blues*. Over the next few years, we should also acquire "St Louis Blues," "Darktown Strutters' Ball," "Twelfth Street Rag," "I Ain't Got Nobody," "Tiger Rag," and many other jazz and blues recordings by such performers as Sophie Tucker, Louis Armstrong, the Original Dixieland Jas Band, Jellyroll Morton, and Jimmy Durante's Jazz Band.

Interestingly, the word *jazz*, at least in the very earliest days, was sometimes written as *jas* or even *jizz*, bespeaking the sexual energy so manifest in this form of music.

The United States, in support of the Allied Powers, would enter the war in 1917. The following spring, the entire 369th Infantry Regiment from New York would be assigned to the French 16th Division. These American soldiers—

most of them Black, a few Puerto Rican—would then be issued French helmets, weapons, belts, and pouches to go with their American uniforms. The regimental nickname of the 369th was the *Black Rattlers*. The name by which they are known today—the *Harlem Hellfighters*—would be bestowed upon them by the enemy they faced in the field. No single unit would be more feared than this one. At the conclusion of the war, a unit citation would be pinned on the regimental colors by General Lebouc, and a hundred seventy individual members of the regiment would be awarded the Croix de Guerre.

The 369th would arrive in France with its own military band, which would march in parades and give free public performances. Their music would be jazz, and it would be well received. Many, like Jean Cocteau, would become almost fanatical aficionados of this new musical form.

CHAPTER 18

The War Years in Paris

At around the time war broke out in Europe (summer of 1914), several of the artists and writers from le Bateau Lavoir—those that did not go into the army—left Montmartre to take up residence at la Ruche. The poet and critic Max Jacob was amongst these.

Incidentally, Max, who hails from Brittany, had been one of the first friends Picasso had found upon his arrival in Paris in 1901. Max had even helped to teach Picasso French, as Dolores and I, a decade later, had taught Marc Chagall. Max usually wrote under his own name, but occasionally he employed various pseudonyms, including *Léon David* and *Morven le Gaëlique*. Let me see. What else can I tell you? Oh, yes. Max painted as well, although somehow, I do not believe that he will ever be remembered for his paintings. But what do I know? I cannot, even today, knowing how much in demand are the works of Picasso, see anything of value in them.

Early in 1915 (the twenty-seventh of February, to be precise), the music hall Moulin Rouge, made famous by Toulouse-Lautrec, burned to the ground. Dolores and I were devastated. Never once had we been inside that establishment, but we knew the outside well. We had drawn it and painted it often.

With its red windmill, Moulin Rouge was Montmartre's best-known landmark. We regarded its loss to be amongst the world's most regrettable disasters.

Eva Gouel, like Modigliani, was afflicted with tuberculosis. When the disease at last claimed her life, Picasso was heartbroken. Mind you, he had, for some months, been carrying on a secret affair with a young model named *Gaby Depeyre*. Very few people were aware of this indiscretion on Picasso's part, but Dolores and I happened to be good friends with Gaby, who confided in us. Picasso eventually would ask her to marry him, but she would refuse, accepting, instead, a like offer from another artist, Herbert Lespinasse. Picasso would then take up with fellow artist Irène Lagut. But this development was still two years in the future.

In November, a young woman named *Adrienne Monnier* opened a bookstore and lending library in the Latin Quarter of the Sixth Arrondissement, the precise address being 7 Rue de l'Odéon. The name of this establishment is *La Maison des Amis des Livres* (or *The House of Friends of Books*). It is within easy walking distance of la Ruche. Dolores and I were two of Adrienne's first customers. We rarely made outright purchases, but we borrowed books regularly. Actually, for the word *borrowed,* you should probably substitute *rented,* for there was associated with book loans a very reasonable fee. Another of Adrienne's loyal customers was Sylvia Beach, a young American woman, who became Adrienne's lover.

During the year 1916, there occurred within the Arts community of Montparnasse four particularly interesting developments of which I must tell you. First, the poet Guillaume Apollinaire received a head wound and was discharged from the army to recover at home. Second, Léonard Foujita divorced the wife he had left in Japan three years earlier. Originally, he had intended to return to Japan after a year or two, but now he had decided to stay in

France indefinitely. He felt it only fair to release his wife from the obligation of waiting chastely for him. Third, Modigliani acquired a new friend and sponsor in the person of Léopold Zborowski, poet and art dealer. And fourth, Nina Hamnett's husband Roald Kristian was deported for being an unregistered alien. I am no longer sure of the order in which these events occurred.

Early in the new year (1917), Georges Braque, recently released from military service after having been wounded in combat, returned to Paris and a hero's welcome. Marie Vassilieff and Max Jacob put their heads together and planned a dinner party in his honor. Amongst the guest were Beatrice Hastings and her latest lover, the sculptor Alfred Pina. Beatrice had but recently ended her two-year affair with Modigliani, who was still smarting from her leaving him. Resentful and prone to violence, Modigliani was not invited to this event. Roaring drunk, he crashed the party anyway. For a few moments, it seemed as though a general mêlée would ensue, but Marie Vassilieff, barely five feet tall, managed to shove Modigliani down the stairs, at which point, Picasso and Manuel Ortiz de Zarate hastened to lock all the doors. The following week, Marie Vassilieff made a drawing of the scuffle just described. It is probably the most-famous of all her artworks.

Two months later, at Café de la Rotonde, Léonard Foujita met Fernande Barrey. He was immediately smitten with her, but she seemed totally unimpressed with him. Refusing to be discouraged, he began a no-holds-barred courtship of her. Thirteen days after their first encounter, they were wed. Fernande, it seemed, had found someone to mentor her as an artist.

Léonard's favorite model at the time was nineteen-year-old Jeanne Hébuterne, who now began posing for Fernande as well. Soon the two young women had become the very best of friends. Dolores and I, who also posed occasionally for Léonard, were, likewise, on friendly terms with Jeanne. Quite often, the four of us (Jeanne, Fernande, Dolores, and I) would meet for coffee.

A female artist for whom we all four posed was sculptor Chana Orloff, who was married to the poet Ary Justman. Through Chana, Jeanne met Modigliani, to whom she promptly gave her heart. Modigliani was equally bewitched with Jeanne.

Leaving la Ruche, Modigliani established an independent studio on Rue de la Grande Chaumière. Jeanne moved in with him, incurring the disfavor of her family. From this point on, the majority of Modigliani's artworks would be likenesses of Jeanne. He settled down some, drank considerably less, and seemed to give up the drugs altogether. Jeanne swore to us that he never once became violent with her.

On the door to Léopold Zborowski's apartment, Modigliani now painted a portrait of Chaim Soutine, who, like Modigliani, was represented by

Zborowski. When Léopold Zborowski and his wife Anna traveled to Nice, they invited Chaim Soutine to accompany them.

In December, Zborowski arranged a one-man show for Modigliani at the Berthe Weill Gallery in Paris. Featured were several nude paintings, which so offended the chief of police that the show was shut down after only a few hours.

Shortly after the first of the year (1918), Dolores came down with Spanish flu and very nearly died. For what seemed to me an eternity, she remained in hospital, delirious with fever. There was really very little that could be done for her, except to make her as comfortable as possible, there being no medicines proven effective against influenza. Neglecting all else, I sat at Dolores's bedside, holding her hand, wiping her brow with a damp cloth, begging her tearfully not to die, and reminding her again and again how much I love her. Why I did not fall ill is anybody's guess.

Not since the Middle Ages had the world faced such a terrifying and widespread epidemic. Over the next two years, between twenty and fifty million lives would be lost as the epidemic asserted itself in four successive waves. Guillaume Apollinaire, only recently recovered from his war wound, succumbed to the flu.

Dolores eventually recovered. On the very day that I was allowed to take her home, we read in the newspaper that Russia had made peace with the Central Powers and would no longer support the Allies or participate in the war. For the entire previous year, Russia had been wracked with revolution and civil war. The czar had abdicated, but it was not entirely clear who was really in control of the government. Indeed, a bitter power struggle seemed to be ongoing.

In the spring, Modigliani and Jeanne left Paris to spend a year in the South of France. There, they paid a call on the aged and arthritic Pierre-Auguste

Renoir, who now lived on a farm near the village of Cagnes-sur-Mer.

By June, it was clear that the war was won. There being so many different nations involved on both sides, there would have to be lots of different treaties, the last of which would not be signed before the end of November. But Peace was returning to Europe.

On the twelfth of July, at the Russian Orthodox Cathedral on Rue Daru, Picasso married Olga Khokhlova, a seventeen-year-old dancer with whom he had recently been sharing an apartment on Rue La Boétie. Dolores and I were invited and attended along with several of our bohemian friends from Montparnasse and Montmartre. Max Jacob and Jean Cocteau signed as witnesses.

Picasso and Olga honeymooned in Biarritz at the villa of Chilean art patron Eugenia Errázuriz. Upon their return to Paris, they moved to a new apartment paid for by the art dealer Paul Rosenberg, who now enjoyed the exclusive right to represent Picasso. Olga frequently invited Dolores and me up for coffee.

The same month that Olga and Picasso were wed, we read in the newspaper that the former Czar of All Russia Nicolas II and his entire family had been murdered by the Bolsheviks, who now appeared to be the predominant power in Russia.

In Nice on the twenty-ninth of November, Jeanne Hébuterne gave birth to a daughter, who was named *Giovanna*.

CHAPTER 19
POST-WAR PARIS

Since our first encounter with Mabel Dodge in 1913, we had stayed in touch, typically exchanging letters with that lady once or twice a year. She was married now to the artist Maurice Sterne with whom she was living in Taos, New Mexico.

This little settlement near a native pueblo had, since the late 1800s, been something of a magnet for artists. Mrs Dodge, who, by the way, refused to adopt her third husband's name, had taken upon herself the challenge of developing Taos into a major art-and-literary colony. She urged every painter, photographer, and writer of her acquaintance to go there and become a full-time resident. The scenery, she promised, was extraordinarily beautiful, the light was exquisite, and the locals were colorful and friendly. For writers, it was a peaceful environment in which to work, and they would enjoy support and inspiration from other creative professionals. "Please come," she urged us. "I'll set you up in a little house of your own."

We were tempted, of course, but we hadn't really got Paris out of our systems yet. "We'll think about it," we promised.

On the nineteenth of November, 1919, Sylvia Beach, with the help of her lover Adrienne Monnier, opened, at 8 Rue Dupuytren, an English-language bookstore, which she called *Shakespeare and Company*. Dolores and I were two of her first customers. Two years later, Shakespeare and Company would relocate to 8 Rue de l'Odéon, directly across the street from Adrienne's own bookstore la Maison des Amis des Livres.

On the twenty-fourth of January, 1920, Modigliani died of tuberculosis. Jeanne, now eight months pregnant with Modigliani's second child, was beside herself with grief and suicidally depressed. Dolores and I did our best to console her, as did, Fernande Barrey. The three of us took turns sitting with her, not daring to let her out of our sight except to visit the bathroom. After dark, Dolores and I returned to our studio, and Fernande made plans to spend the night with Jeanne. The baby was with Jeanne's parents.

After midnight, Dolores and I were awakened by a frantic Fernande. "Hurry! Get dressed. You've got to help me find her. She gave me the slip. I just dozed off for a moment, and she was gone."

"The bridges!" Dolores suggested as she pulled on a heavy coat.

The nearest bridge was Pont des Arts, a pedestrian bridge spanning the Seine from Sixth to First Arrondissement. If we did not find Jeanne there, we should then split up, Fernande going upriver to the next bridge, Dolores and I heading downriver.

We were out of breath when we arrived, but we were in luck. In the very center of the bridge, Jeanne could be seen as immobile as a statue. She was poised on the rail gazing into the dark waters below. We hurried to her as silently as possible, fearful of startling her into jumping or causing her to lose her balance. Fernande reached her first and helped her down. By the time Dolores and I caught up, Jeanne was crying and apologizing for being so inconsiderate.

"I'm so ashamed of myself," she sniffled. "What kind of friend am I to cause you three such concern and bring you out in the cold on a night like this?"

Early the following morning Jeanne's parents collected her and took her into their care. The day after that, Jeanne threw herself out of a window in her parents' fifth-floor apartment, killing herself and her unborn infant.

Fernande, Dolores, and I then drank ourselves into a stupor. It was the only way we felt able deal with the tragedy.

Fernande was still married to Léonard Foujita. He had instructed her and helped her to get her art career off the ground. At the urging of Chaim Soutine, she had also taken classes at École Nationale Supérieure des Beaux-Arts. She was now quite accomplished and was regularly selling pictures through some of the same galleries that handled her husband's paintings.

Fernande and Léonard's marriage, by the way, was what might be described as *non-exclusive monogamy.* By mutual consent, they both had numerous lovers.

In the spring, Dolores and I agreed that we had finally had enough of Paris. Jeanne's suicide still weighed heavily on our hearts. Before the worst heat and humidity of summer could set in, we meant to take our leave. I wrote to Mabel Dodge, asking if her offer of a house could still be counted on. In less than a month, we heard back from her. Enclosed in Mrs Dodge's letter were snapshots of a little adobe dwelling that was to be ours. We made steam-ship reservations and began crating up all our unsold artworks for shipment to our new address. Then we made the rounds, saying our *goodbyes* to everyone we knew in Montparnasse, Montmartre, and the Latin Quarter. Both Fernande Barrey and Miss Toklas made us promise to write frequently, and they, in turn, promised to keep us informed of events in Paris.

CHAPTER 20

THE TAOS ART COLONY

The little house that Mabel Dodge had picked out for us was of adobe construction, quite plain, and very, very old. Mind you, we found it as immaculate as a hospital. It was freshly repainted inside and out. The nearby Kit Carson house, by the way, was a near-perfect match to ours, and that dwelling, which had once been the home of the great frontiersman, was known to have been built in 1825. It seemed likely that our house dated from the same era.

We were delighted to discover that, besides Mrs Dodge, we already had other friends here. The cubist painter Andrew Dasburg had arrived from Paris in 1918. There, we had known him only to say *hello* in passing; here, he embraced us as his own long-lost sisters. From our days in New York City, we were casually acquainted with painters Mary Shepard Greene and her husband Ernest Blumenschein. They too now treated us as the dearest of old friends.

Incidentally, Ernest claimed to have been the first artist ever to have discovered Taos back in 1898. Since then, he had made frequent summer trips to paint here. In 1919, he and Mary had settled here permanently.

A new friend for us was Elsie Clews Parsons, an anthropologist whose special interest was Native American cultures.

As for Mrs Dodge, her third marriage was already in shambles. Separated from her husband artist Maurice Sterne, she was living now with Native

American artist Tony Luhan. Once her divorce became final, she and Tony would wed, and this time she would take her husband's name. She would, in 1923, become *Mabel Dodge Luhan, Dodge* being the name of her second husband. Her birth name was *Mabel Ganson.* Her husbands, in their proper order, were Karl Evans, Edwin Dodge, Maurice Sterne, and finally Tony Luhan.

In the autumn of 1921, a letter from Fernande Barrey informed us that her former lover, the photographer Jean Agélou, and his brother Georges had died in an automobile accident on the twenty-first of August.

The following day, a letter from Miss Toklas mentioned that Fernande's husband Tsuguharu Foujita, whom Dolores and I knew as *Léonard,* was currently engaged in an affair with a model named Lucie Badoul. "He calls her *Youki,* which, I understand, means *Snow Rose.* She is his latest muse. Mademoiselle Fernande has lovers of her own; she is a muse to many."

Dolores reminded me that Picasso too was given to renaming whomever he was enamoured of at the moment.

We still maintained an infrequent correspondence with Robert Henri, who had been our mentor and instructor years ago in Greenwich Village. During the summer of 1922, we called on him in Santa Fe, where he was spending a few months painting desert landscapes and portraits of Native Americans. It was wonderful to see him again. Before returning to Taos, we also paid visits to several art galleries, one of which we consigned painting to.

In September, the English author DH Lawrence and his wife Frieda, accepting a long-standing invitation from Mabel Dodge, arrived in Taos to take up residence here. I had never been a particular fan of DH Lawrence, but I was somewhat familiar with his writings, having read (without much enjoyment, I must admit) *Sons and Lovers* and *The Rainbow*.

What I had not known and now learned was that the writer was also an artist. He signed his paintings *Lorenzo.* I believe that Dolores and I were the only women in Taos not in love with him. They flocked around him, competing for his attention, each one wanting to think of herself as his muse. It was laughable really. *Lorenzo* is how we came to know him and how we addressed him. On the evening of the eleventh, we attended a dinner party at Mrs Dodge's home, the occasion being Lorenzo's thirty-seventh birthday.

The following year, Lorenzo and Frieda traveled back to England, only to return to Taos a short time later. That same year, they were visited briefly by the English artist Dorothy Brett, and at some point—I cannot remember exactly when—by the writer Aldous Huxley.

Another letter from Miss Toklas informed us that Marc Chagall was now back in Paris, and with him was his wife Bella, "an absolutely delightful young lady, charming, biddable, and quite pretty." Leaving what was now the Soviet Union, they had traveled first to Berlin in hopes of recovering the paintings Marc had consigned to a dealer there in 1914. Unfortunately, that man could not be located; the painting were, therefore, assumed to be lost.

In 1924, Mrs Dodge, hoping to entice Lorenzo into staying permanently in Taos, offered to give him a little ranch of a hundred sixty acres. Lorenzo declined. But Frieda accepted, and so Lobo Ranch was deeded to her. Located some eighteen miles outside of town, this property had two little shacks on it, no electricity and no running water. Lorenzo and Frieda made one of these shacks their home. Dorothy Brett, returning to Taos, moved into the second shack and served Lorenzo as his secretary. Lobo Ranch was then renamed *Kiowa Ranch.*

Mrs Dodge has claimed that she did not give the ranch to the Lawrences but sold it to them, the price being the original manuscript of *Sons and Lovers,* which she does indeed possess, but I believe that it was gifted to her by Lorenzo after the fact and not as a condition of the land transfer.

Whilst abiding in Taos, Lorenzo and Frieda traveled frequently to Oaxaca. On one such trip in 1925, Lorenzo contracted malaria. He was already suffering from tuberculosis. His health was very delicate. His recovery from malaria was painfully slow. When he was able to travel again, he and Frieda moved to Florence, Italy, which they believed would be better for Lorenzo's health.

Dorothy Brett remained alone on the ranch for a couple of weeks. The first time she came into Taos to shop, Dolores and I offered to put her up at our house until she could find a place of her own in town. Eventually, she rented a hut next to the home of Frank Waters.

To support herself, she did what others in Taos (myself included) had already begun doing. We sold pictures to tourists at prices so low that we were forced to be incredibly prolific in order to survive. The quality of my paintings suffered, but somehow, this new way of working, gave Dorothy's paintings a mystical quality that was very appealing and soon made her famous.

Dolores, refusing to compromise, kept painting exactly as she always had, but because she was selling fewer pictures these days, she raised her prices.

Letters from Miss Toklas and from Fernande kept us abreast of goings-on in Paris. We learned from Miss Toklas that Fernande and Léonard had finally split up. Apparently, Fernande had enjoyed one particular affair that Léonard was unwilling or unable to forgive, that being with his cousin Koyanagi, a painter.

"I've never heard of this Koyanagi," Dolores interrupted my reading the letter aloud. "Have you?"

"Nope," I said and resumed reading.

It seemed that, after divorcing Fernande, Léonard had married his muse, the one he called *Youki* or *Snow Rose*. Fernande was now living with Koyanagi.

Another letter, this one from Fernande contained an amusing story about Marc Chagall and Chaim Soutine. Inspired by Rembrandt's painting *The Slaughtered Ox,* which he had seen in the Louvre, Chaim acquired a beef carcass, which he hung in his studio and began a series of ten paintings of it.

Marc noticed blood on the floor seeping under the door to Chaim's studio and became alarmed. Dashing out into the street, he shouted, "Someone has killed Soutine."

Nor was this even the end of the story. Neighbors began complaining about the stench, and the police came to Chaim's studio to demand that the carcass be removed. Chaim immediately launched into an impassioned lecture on the value of art over hygiene and on the sanctity of the artistic process. Amazingly, the young *flic* was persuaded. He apologized and went away. The stinking carcass remained in place.

In 1926, Taos was paid a visit by fine-art photographer Paul Strand and his British-born wife Rebecca Salsbury, a painter. They stayed, of course, with Mrs Dodge (now *Mrs Luhan*). Rebecca and Paul both exhibited and sold their works at Alfred Stieglitz's art gallery called *291*, where Dolores and I had once bought two fine-art photographs. Stieglitz and his wife Georgia O'Keeffe were close friends of the Strands. In a letter to Stieglitz and O'Keeffe, Rebecca urged them to come sometime to Taos, adding that Georgia would "do great things here."

Three years later, Rebecca returned to Taos, and with her, she brought her friend Georgia O'Keeffe.

That same year, 1929, the Queen of Montparnasse, Alice Prin, now age twenty-eight, published her autobiography titled *Kiki's Memoirs*. Léonard (Tsuguharu Foujita) had written an introduction for it. Dolores and I made a special trip to Santa Fe to buy a copy of Kiki's book.

The following year, DH Lawrence died of tuberculosis. Frieda returned to

New Mexico to live at Kiowa Ranch, bearing her husband's ashes with her. Mrs Luhan argued that those ashes should be scattered here at Taos. That was Lorenzo's expressed desire, she claimed. She seemed quite determined to have her way. Frieda was having none of it. I believe that she was actually afraid that Mrs Luhan would somehow manage to steal the ashes. To prevent any possibility of that's happening, she mixed the ashes into wet cement, which was then cast into a great block of concrete to serve as a permanent monument at Kiowa Ranch.

CHAPTER 21

A Slight Depression

With the stock market crash of last October, the country seems to have fallen into a deep economic recession. Mind you, some politicians are insisting that this is not really a proper recession, but only a "slight depression." By whatever name it is called, it has ordinary people afraid to spend money on anything non-essential, including works of art.

Of course, ordinary people are not usually the ones who buy from us anyway. Even if we price our creations so low that school teachers, policemen, firefighters, grocers, pharmacists, and cobblers can easily afford to buy from us, they do so but rarely. We artists, I hate to admit, are largely dependent upon the acquisitiveness of wealthy collectors for our survival and for our ability to continue to make art.

President Hoover, in March of this year, assured the public that the worst of this recession was now behind us. I wish that I could believe his estimation of the situation to be accurate. Admittedly, I know very little about the science of economics, but my instinct is warning me to prepare for a long siege. I guess we shall know soon enough.

In any event, Dolores and I put in a vegetable garden back in the spring and bought a few goats, which we have learned to milk. We even make our own cheese now. Others in town have taken similar steps. The byword on everyone's lips these days is *self-sufficiency*.

Letters from Clovis, who is still in England and is still with David, warn that another war is becoming more and more likely with every passing year. Germany's unreasonable desire for hegemony, Clovis asserts, was the primary cause of the last war and will be the cause of the next. Why is it, I wonder, that nations seek to exercise power over their neighbor states? Why cannot nations get along together in a friendly way, as do individuals of a village?

Now, before I close this narrative, I must mention that Dolores and I—she always insists that I accompany her when she travels—visit her family in Oklahoma at least twice a year and have done so since our moving to Taos nearly a decade ago.

And finally, museums on both coasts have recently acquired paintings by Dolores. Her talent and her genius, which I recognized more than twenty years ago, are now becoming known to the world. I could not be more pleased.

THE END

About the Author

Madeleine Whitecrow Ashe was born in Mexico City to expatriate parents. Her father is British; her mother, American of mixed race (Hispanic and Navajo). Ms Ashe is the author of two other books of historical fiction: *Scouting for the Texians: Manuela Ballardo's Recollections of her Exploits and Adventures* and *Autobiography of Bat Masterson.* She is currently working on another historical novel, tentatively titled *Little Durango,* which will be about the taming of the Arizona Borderlands (1869 – 1900).

www.ingramcontent.com/pod-product-compliance
Lightning Source LLC
La Vergne TN
LVHW090948080826
845145LV00003B/929

* 9 7 8 1 7 3 4 7 8 1 4 1 0 *